written by Pat Mora

illustrated by Alyssa Bermudez



MAGINATION PRESS • WASHINGTON, DC

American Psychological Association

*For my treasured sister, Stella Mora Henry, who wisely assisted thousands of families with the challenges of aging—***PM**

*For all of the forgotten memories and cherished ones yet to come—***AB**

Magination Press is a registered trademark of the American Psychological Association. Order books at maginationpress.org, or call 1-800-374-2721.

Book design by Susan K. White
Printed by Worzalla, Stevens Point, WI

Library of Congress Cataloging-in-Publication Data
Names: Mora, Pat, author. | Bermudez, Alyssa, illustrator.
Title: My singing Nana / by Pat Mora ; illustrated by Alyssa Bermudez.
Description: Washington, DC : Magination Press, [2019] | "American Psychological Association." | Summary: Billy's beloved Nana's memory is failing but they are "always amigos," so when disaster strikes the day of the family's big summer show, Billy finds a way he and Nana can save the day.
Identifiers: LCCN 2018038336| ISBN 9781433830211 (hardcover) | ISBN 1433830213 (hardcover)
Subjects: | CYAC: Grandmothers—Fiction. | Family life—Fiction. | Alzheimer's disease—Fiction. | Revues—Fiction. | Hispanic Americans—Fiction.
Classification: LCC PZ7.M78819 My 2019 | DDC [E]—dc23 LC record available at https://lccn.loc.gov/2018038336

Manufactured in the United States of America
10 9 8 7 6 5 4 3 2 1

"Can I roll the pie dough, Nana?"
I ask. I'm Nana's helper.
We're making cherry empanadas,
Dad's favorite.
Nana hums when she cooks.

She likes to sing too.
She winks and sings,

"Can she bake an empanada, Billy Boy, Billy Boy?"

Nana's wink makes me smile.
She says that's my song because my name is Billy.

Becky and Chris, my little sister and brother, dance around the kitchen singing,

"Billy Boy, Billy Boy."

Becky asks, "Nana, can I sprinkle the sugar on the empanadas?"

"Can I eat an empanada?" asks Chris.

Soon the kitchen smells delicious, a red cherry smell.

After dinner, I say, “Empanada time!”

Dad tastes his first bite slowly. “Umm!” he says.

Nana pats my shoulder. “Billy helped me bake the empanadas,” she says.

Nana and I like putting on shows
for our family and friends.
We started when I was three.
Nana is the director.
Tomorrow is our summer
show, and Dad and I
have the patio ready
with balloons and
surprises. We
even have a
little stage.

"Tomorrow will be our best show ever, right Nana?" I ask. "Tonight's our last chance to practice."

"Remind me, Billy, what are we doing this year?" asks Nana.

I look at Mom. "Remember, Nana," I say. "I'm going to read the story I wrote about a boy giant who saves animals."

"I'm going to play my drums," says Chris, drumming on the table.

"And I'm going to sing," says Becky.

Nana gives Becky a big abrazo. “What song are you singing, querida?”
“I’m singing the song you wrote for me, ‘La Señorita Bonita,’” says Becky.

Becky and Chris jump up
and salsa around the room.

Nana sings "La Señorita Bonita"
with Becky. We practice our show,
and Nana, Mom, and Dad clap.
Nana takes my hand. "Billy, sometimes
your Nana forgets things, but we help each
other, don't we? I ask you your spelling
words, and you help me remember things."

Nana and I smack our palms together and say,

"Always amigos!"

When Mom tucks me in, she asks,
"What's the matter, Billy?"

"I'm worried about Nana," I say.
"She's forgetting things. Is she OK?
What if she forgets our show? She's the director."

"I know," says Mom, putting her arm around me,
"Nana is forgetting some things."

Mom says she took Nana to the doctor. The doctor asked Nana some questions. "The doctor said that Nana sometimes needs our help," says Mom.

"Can Nana still play with Becky, Chris, and me?" I ask.

"Sure, she can play and roll dough and sing with you," says Mom. "What else do you like to do with Nana?"

Billy
Rocks

“Lots of things,” I say. “I like to show Nana my rock collection, and I like to eat ice cream with her. I like to sing with her and listen to her sing to her plants.  I like to sit close to Nana when she reads me a book. Sometimes I read her books too.”

Mom gives me a big hug. “We all love Nana, and she loves us. Your hugs make Nana happy. Big day tomorrow,” says Mom. “¿Un besito? Time for bed.”

The next morning, Becky whispers, “Billy, I can’t talk. My throat hurts.”
She starts coughing and coughing.
“Mom!” I say. “Come quick. Becky’s sick.”
“Oh no!” I think. “What if we can’t do the show?”

Dad makes Becky some hot té de canela.

"I'm sorry your throat hurts, Becky," I say. "I just wanted to do our show."

Chris plays a soft drum song for Becky.

“What’s the matter, Billy?” asks Nana when she sees me.

“Becky’s sick, Nana, and we can’t do our show. There’s no singer.”

Nana takes my hand. “Let’s go see her,” says Nana.
“Maybe she’ll feel better later.”

Becky spends the morning curled in Nana's lap
while the family gets ready for our summer show.

Before lunch, we all hold hands around the table and bow our heads. "Billy," says Mom. "What are you thankful for today?"

"I'm thankful for my Nana," I say. "She's sweeter than cherry empanadas."

Nana smiles and blows me a kiss. "Gracias, mi querido," she says.

Friends and family begin to arrive. I try to smile at everyone, but I feel nervous. Who's going to sing after I read my story?

When everyone sits down, Nana whispers,
"Billy, stand up, bow, and start reading."

"But then what?" I whisper.

"Stand up, bow, and start reading, querido," says Nana.
"Our audience is waiting."

I stand and begin my new story: "Once there was
a boy named Billy who was bigger than a dinosaur."
Chris bangs and bangs his drums.

When I finish my story, everyone claps, and I bow.
Then, I look at everyone. I see Nana smiling at me,
and I have an idea. I know who the best singer is.

I reach out and take Nana's hand. She smiles and comes to stand by me. We hold hands. Nana and I look at each other and smile. Then, we start to sing together.

I help Nana and she helps me remember our favorite songs in Spanish and English. She sings and sings and soon everyone is singing, and Nana is directing. We sing “La Señorita Bonita” too. When everyone claps, Chris beats his drums loudly, and Becky claps and claps.

I look up at Nana. Her eyes are smiling.
I give her a big abrazo and smell
her perfume. We smack our
palms together and say,

"Always amigos!"

# Author Note

Families savor happy memories. A number of the women in my family were wonderful cooks, and I enjoyed having my three children help me bake. Soon, my granddaughter will be my helper. Baking memories and family gatherings are happy memories for us. All families, of course, confront challenging realities too including aging.

How do children respond to grandparents or other seniors who may begin to experience memory loss, and where do children have opportunities to share and discuss their confusion, worries, and feelings?

In their eighties, both of my parents suffered from dementia. Alzheimer's, named for the German physician, Dr. Alois Alzheimer, who first identified the brain disorder that now bears his name, is the most common form of dementia. Not a normal part of aging, Alzheimer's is regularly in the news, since an estimated 5.8 million Americans are confronting this disease, according to the Alzheimer's Association.

I was encouraged to write this book by my sister, Stella Henry, who cared for our parents at the end of their lives. For over thirty years, as a nurse, administrator, and co-owner of a nursing home, she helped thousands of families deal with challenging health issues.

Caring adults know that children are capable of compassion and thoughtfulness. A few reminders:

- Be truthful with children. Share age-appropriate information.

- Encourage children to share their worries with parents and trusted family members or teachers. Children's questions provide clues about appropriate issues to address with a child and her or his level of understanding.

- Remind children to be polite and patient with their family member or friend.

- Model loving, thoughtful behavior that strengthens family bonds.

I often smile at many happy memories of my parents and think of my teasing dad and my mom's fabulous laugh.

# Nana's Cherry Empanadas

*Makes 8-10 empanadas*

DOUGH:

1 large (8 oz.) package of cream cheese
½ tsp. salt
1 stick butter (8 tablespoons)
2 c. flour

Cut the cream cheese and butter into about 1-inch cubes. Add 4 Tbsp water. Gradually add salt and flour to the cream cheese and butter mixture, stirring to combine. Knead the dough until the ingredients are combined and dough is just a little bit sticky. Form the dough mixture into a ball and wrap it well in plastic wrap. Refrigerate it for 30 minutes to half a day to ease rolling. While the dough is chilling, you can make your filling.

FILLING:

You can use preserves, canned pie filling, or make your own. My children liked the following cherry filling:

1 can (14.5 oz) sour cherries
dash of cinnamon
½ c. sugar (plus extra for sprinkling)
⅛ tsp. almond extract
2 Tbsp. flour

Cook cherries, sugar, and flour over low heat on the stovetop, stirring occasionally, until thickened. Add remaining ingredients and stir. Allow the filling to cool completely before filling the empanadas.

Roll out dough on well-floured surface as thin as possible without it tearing, about ¼ inch thick. Use a round cookie or biscuit cutter to cut the dough into circles about 5-6 inches wide. If you don't have a cutter, tracing a knife around a plastic lid can be used in a pinch.

Spoon a tablespoon of filling slightly off-center of the pastry circles, leaving enough room around the filling to completely close the empanada. Moisten the pastry edges with water if needed and fold the dough over the filling, gently forming half-circle shaped empanadas. Press the edges lightly with floured fork tines to seal.

BAKE:

Bake the empanadas on an ungreased cookie sheet at 375° about 20-25 minutes or until golden. Before you bake, you can sprinkle with sugar or cinnamon-sugar, or after they are baked, but still warm, you can dredge the empanadas in sugar.

Serve warm with a scoop of vanilla ice cream if you like! You can also serve the empanadas at room temperature.

## About the Author

**PAT MORA** has published over thirty-five books that have earned immense praise. Her recent books include *Bookjoy, Wordjoy; The Remembering Day/ El día de los muertos;* and *Water Rolls, Water Rises/El agua rueda, el agua sube*. Her titles have appeared on the ALA Notable Books list, the Texas Bluebonnet Master List, been awarded Pura Belpré honors, been placed on the Notable Books for a Global Society list, and have been honored by the International Latino Book Awards, the Tomás Rivera Mexican American Children's Book Awards, the Americas Book Awards, and much more. A literacy advocate excited about sharing what she calls "bookjoy," she founded the annual Children's Day, Book Day—in Spanish, El día de los niños, El día de los libros, "Día." Pat is a popular speaker about creativity, inclusivity, and bookjoy. She is always working on new books. She lives in Santa Fe, New Mexico. Visit patmora.com and @patmora_author on Twitter.

## About the Illustrator

**ALYSSA BERMUDEZ** is a born-and-bred New Yorker living down under in Tassie! She studied illustration and animation at the Fashion Institute of Technology. As an illustrator and art teacher for students aged 5–75+, she strives to put the *KA-POW* into stories and learning. She illustrated the popular "Lucia the Luchadora" and "Amelia Chamelia" series. Her work can be found amongst books, fabrics, walls, and beyond. She currently resides in stunning Hobart, Australia where adventures await each day. Visit alyssabermudezart.com and @bermudezbahama on Twitter and Instagram.

## About Magination Press

**MAGINATION PRESS** is the children's book imprint of the American Psychological Association. Through APA's publications, the association shares with the world mental health expertise and psychological knowledge. Magination Press books reach young readers and their parents and caregivers to make navigating life's challenges a little easier. It's the combined power of psychology and literature that makes a Magination Press book special. Visit maginationpress.org.